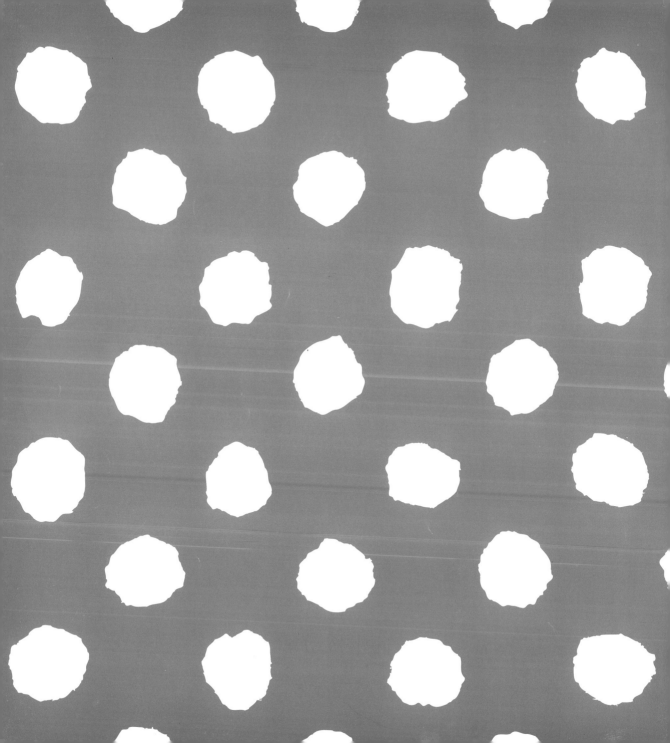

little blue and little yellow

a story for Pippo and Ann

and other children

by Leo Lionni

HarperCollinsPublishers

Little blue and little yellow
Copyright © 1959 by Leo Lionni
Printed in the U.S.A. All rights reserved.
Published by arrangement with Astor-Honor Publishing, Inc.

Library of Congress Cataloging-in-Publication Data
Lionni, Leo.
  Little blue and little yellow / Leo Lionni.
    p.   cm.
  Summary: A little blue spot and a little yellow spot are best friends, and when they hug each other they become green.
  ISBN 0-688-13285-5
  [1. Color—Fiction.   2. Friendship—Fiction.] I. Title.
PZ7.L6634Li   1995   94-7324
[E]—dc20   CIP
                                              AC

Visit us on the World Wide Web!
www.harperchildrens.com

This is little blue.

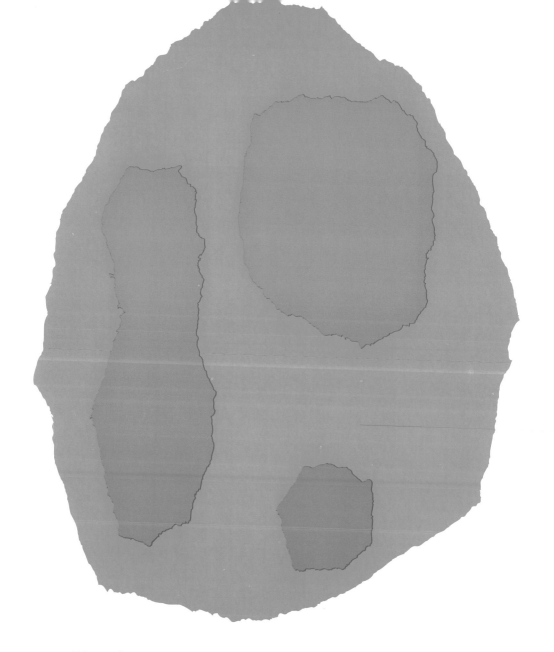

Here he is at home with papa and mama blue.

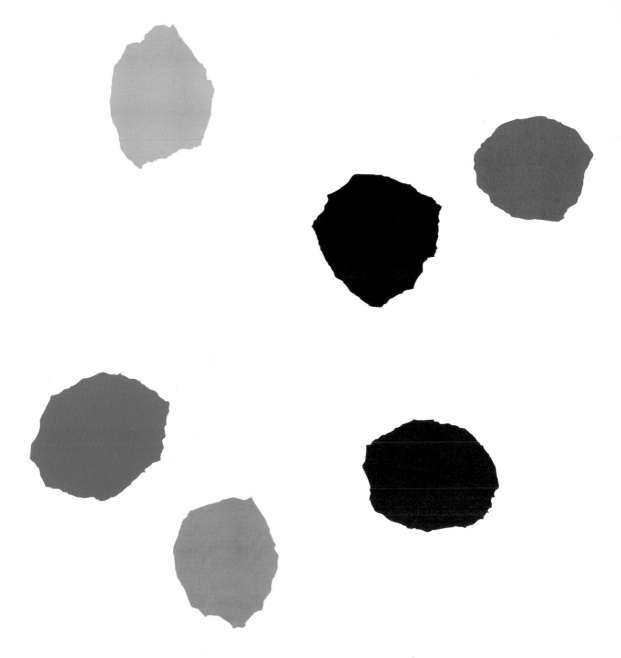

Little blue has many friends

but his best friend is little yellow

who lives across the street.

How they love to play at *Hide-and-Seek*

and *Ring-a-Ring-O' Roses!*

In school they sit still in neat rows.

After school they run and jump.

One day mama blue went shopping. "You stay home" she said to little bl

But little blue went out to look for little yellow.

Alas! The house across the street was empty.

He looked here

and there

and everywhere... until suddenly, around a corner...

there was little yellow!

Happily they hugged each other

and hugged each other

until they were green.

Then they went to play in the park.

They ran through a tunnel.

They chased little orange.

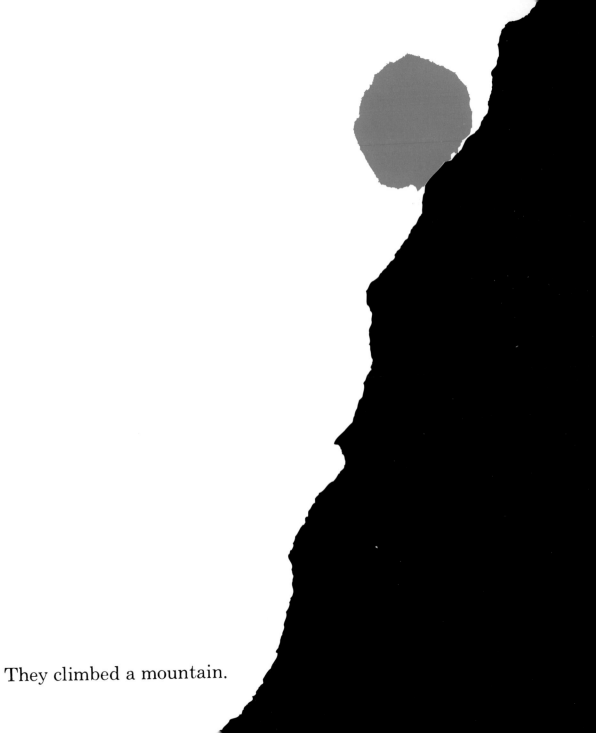

They climbed a mountain.

When they were tired

they went home.

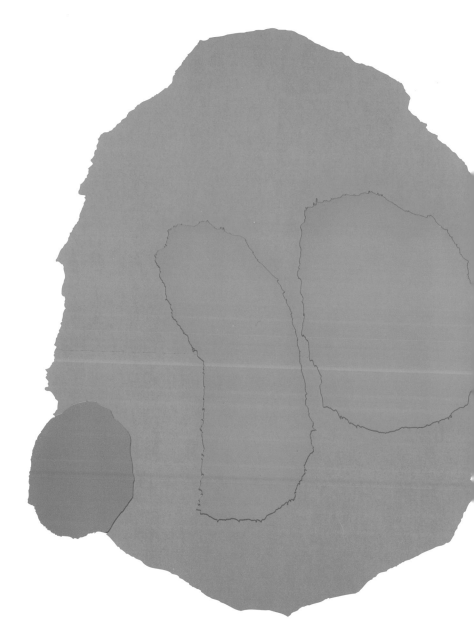

But papa and mama blue said: "You are not our little blue—you are green."

d papa and mama yellow said: "You are not our little yellow—you are green."

Little blue and little yellow were very sad. They cried big blue and yellow te

They cried and cried until they were *all* tears.

When they finally pulled themselves together they said: "Will they
believe us
now?"

Mama blue and papa blue were very happy to see their little blue.

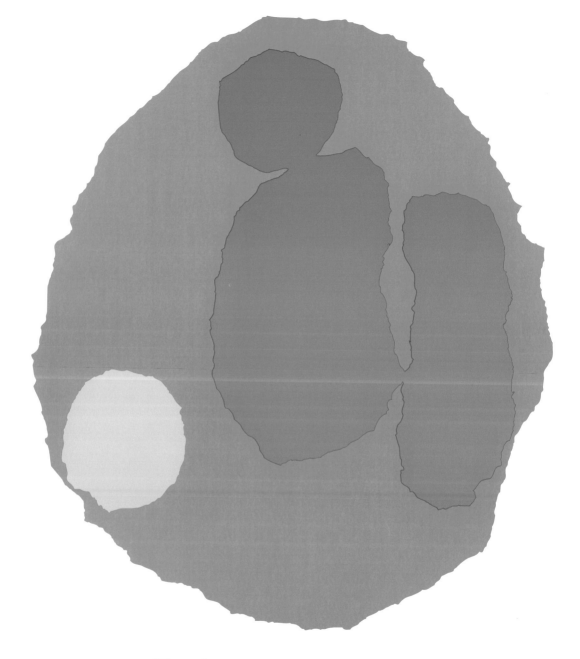

They hugged and kissed him

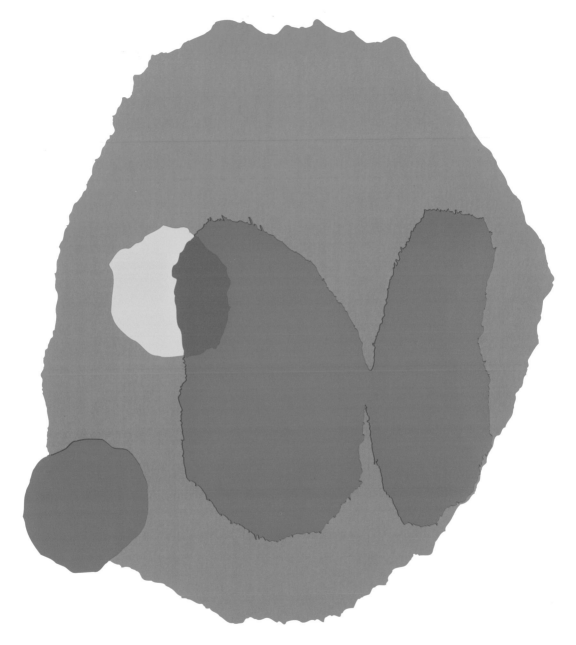

And they hugged little yellow too...but look . . . they became green!

Now they knew what had happened

and so they went across the street to bring the good news.

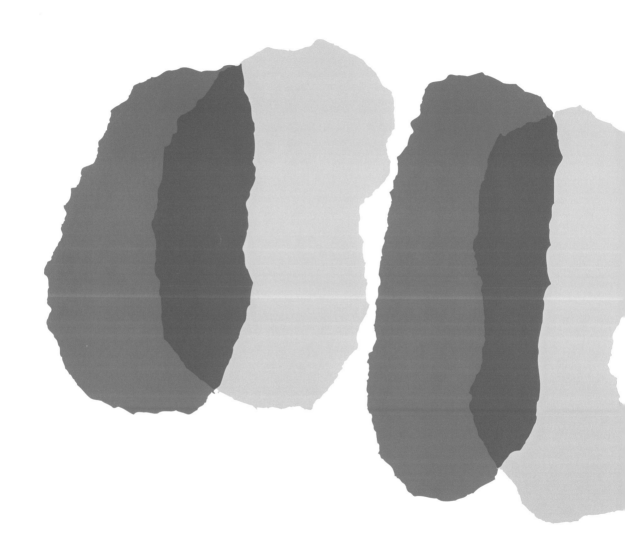

They all hugged each other with joy

and the children played until suppertime.

The End

More Picture Books
by Leo Lionni

Inch by Inch. A winning, winsome inchworm is proud of his ability to measure just about anything under the sun—and then some. (ISBN 0-688-13283-9)

On My Beach There Are Many Pebbles. Challenge young readers to look closely at the most ordinary of objects to discover the extraordinary beauty and majesty of each. (ISBN 0-688-13284-7)